SARZCROSANCT

A PLAY

SARZCROSANCT

A PLAY

EMMANUEL OLABAYO

ISBN: 978-978-769-800-6

Published in Nigeria in 2024 by LIBRETTO Publishers

LIBRETTO PUBLISHERS LIMITED
HEADOFFICE
Office R7, Owode, Lagos Garage,
Shopping Complex, Oyo, Oyo State, Nigeria.

BRANCHES
Edo | Abuja
Tel: +234 (0) 807 834 6790 | +234 (0) 813 044 6615
Email: librettong@gmail.com | publishing@librettong.com | info@librettong.com
Website: www.librettong.com | Bookstore Website: www.books.librettong.com
facebook.com/librettopublish | instagram.com/libretto_ng |
twitter.com/librettopublish | linkedin.com/company/libretto-publishers-ltd

Cover Design by Dhee Sylvester
Book Layout and Design and Typesetting by Nosakhare Collins
Printed and Bound in Nigeria by Libretto Publishers Limited

To young men and women who were legit, yet had their lives cut short by those who should protect them.

To parents, guardians and other family members, forced to mourn their wards.

To innocent kids who were brought to this world, but never met those that brought them because they were killed extra judicially.

To patriots who gave their lives, just so others could live.

To activists and voices, who are right in the thick of the #EndSARZ campaign.

To every young Nigerian trying to make an honest living, but have been embarrassed and discouraged by the men in Black.

To the few officers of the Force who have refused to compromise, but victimized by the lots.

Author's Notes

"If your enemy is secure at all points, be prepared for him. If he is in superior strength, evade him. If your opponent is temperamental, seek to irritate him. Pretend to be weak, that he may grow arrogant. If he is taking his ease, give him no rest. If his forces are united, separate them. If sovereign and subject are in accord, put division between them. Attack him where he is unprepared, appear where you are not expected." –Sun Tzu, *The Art of War.*

The security of life and properties are extremely important. If members of a society are confident in the security systems put in place by their leaders at all levels, the result will be evident in the development of the society, especially in such areas as the economy, security and infrastructure. This primarily was what informed The Nigerian Police to come up with a unit sometime in 1997, called SPECIAL ANTI-ROBBERY SQUAD (SARS). At that time, arm robbery and kidnapping were the order of the day. The unit was effective in tackling these security challenges, especially under a Military

Junta, and was successful at restoring sanity to the society.

With the advancements of technology came new ways for criminals to beat the system and commit crimes. The explosion of financial crimes coincided with the advent of the internet as criminals exploited quick communication to rip people off their monies. And so, SARS had an extra layer of burden on their already heavy shoulder – cybercrime. Although SARS, as referenced in Majek Fashek's song, *Police Brutality,* were menace to the citizens, their new responsibilities added feathers to a dangerous birds' flight.

It is with these new responsibilities that the SARS unit transformed from a security agency to a security threat. Like Sun Tzu said in the above quote, "If your enemy is in superior strength, evade him." For many Nigerians today, this is the reality. At the sight of members of SARS, they simply disappear into thin air.

SARS officers are funded with taxpayers' money to protect citizens, so it is unfortunate they use their positions and ammunition to threaten people they're to protect. In the last two years, many have been unlucky, unable to escape from SARS death-grip.

In 2019 alone, more than a dozen Nigerians died to SARS bullets. The growing terror SARS caused was becoming one too many that Nigerians decided to rise to the occasion.

SARS killings were so sporadic that you can be doing nothing so random but still meet your demise from their bullets. The randomness of their killings is typified when, in April 2019, one Kolade Johnson, was shot while he came out of viewing centre. One is almost made to ask if watching football in a public space has become a crime.

For Chinedu Obi, aka Zinquest, a hip-hop artist, his end came when SARS officers accosted him for spotting tattoos. He was shot dead on the spot. There was another case of a bus driver in the Magboro area of Lagos State who was shot at and eventually died for refusing to part away with his own money. It was also reported in the news of how a young man, a commercial motorcycle rider (Okada), was shot dead during an argument with a Police officer over #100. While editing this work, it was reported that a SARS officer killed a professional football player, Tiamiyu Kazeem who played for Remo Stars, Sagamu, Ogun State. Members of the community took to the street to protest the killing of Tiamiyu, however, men of NPF attacked them and more killings were recorded. These are just a few examples of civilians who became a prey in the hands of those saddled with the responsibilities to protect them.

The question, therefore, has been: what is the Government doing to curb this fast-growing menace? If the primary assignment of a government is to protect lives and properties, then it is failing, and failing woefully.

Citizens have been calling for a police reform, and a total overhauling of the SARS Unit. #EndSARS trends at least once a month on all major Social Media platforms, in the past 3 years. This clearly shows the high rate and frequency of the atrocities members of this Unit commit. The SARS Department (mostly all tactical squads) of the Force still continues to be brutal and irresponsible even after some sort of partial reform was championed by the Government, which saw a change in name from SARS to F-SARS and reviewed operations.

This play is an attempt at raising such questions as; are members of the SARS Unit (tactical squads of the Police and the police formation itself) and their operations SACROSANCT? Is every young Nigerian, especially males, into Yahoo Yahoo (Internet Scamming)? Are young ladies with smart phones prostitutes? Where do we go from here? What do we do? These questions are salient, and we must find answers to these questions before it is too late.

While we have come a long way, and significant successes have been recorded in this quest, the truth remains that we still have a longer way to go. This is a fight that we must see to the end. If the campaign has survived three years (which is probably the longest of any of such) then it is capable of surviving many more years until the goal is achieved – to have a Police that works for the people. While we continue to fight this battle, we must keep our young men and women safe. We must also realize the importance of coming together to fight this enemy that is now common to all of us, one that has become a national threat.

P.S: For arts' sake, we will use SARZ instead of SARS.

Dramatis personae

NARRATOR	Young man/lady in his/her early twenties.
FUNMI AGUNBIADE	In his late twenties or early thirties. A passionate musician, uncompromising Police officer and very determined young man.
SOGUNLE	Of the same age as FUNMI, and his closest friend. He is Street Smart but carefree about life.
DPO	In his early fifties, stereotypical Nigerian Police Officer – chubby, big stomach that he struggles to hide under his big sized uniform.
OFFICER 1	Typical Nigerian Police front desk officer, roughly dressed in his uniform and an award-winning talker.
OFFICER 2	Can be played by a male or female actor. Partner to OFFICER 1 at the front desk, with attributes of a gossip.

OFFICER JAMES	In his early forties, appears clean and sharp in his uniform, laced with black shades, and tactically corrupt officer.
BOY 1, 2 & 3	Same as the characters in the Montages, young men who are sometimes loud in their dressing and rash in their actions, yet, legit and hard workers.
LADY	Young and sophisticated.
VOICE 1, 2, 3 & 4	Males and females who are freedom fighters, bold and daring.
DANCERS	Members of the Orchestra
MOB	Members of the Orchestra

Sets

The play has two main locales, FUNMI's house on stage right and the POLICE STATION on stage left. The apron is better suited for the street scenes. The play also uses a style that allows constant communication with actors and members of the orchestra. For the Montages, however, the entire stage would be appropriate while lights and sound clearly shows the time and place of actions. The straight take technique is suggested in order to keep and sustain the tempo of the play. Deliberate blackout can be used, if not, songs and stage hands should be used in scene transitions.

Note to the Director

If it is possible victims of SARZ, especially those dead, should be recognized. You will find a few names mentioned in the opening notes. Also note that this play was written before the #ENDSARZ campaign moved from online to the streets of Nigeria. Therefore, the events of the street protests as they originally played out are not documented here. However, it will be great if the director can reference victims of the #ENDSARZ offline protest, particularly those of the Lekki massacre of 20th October, 2020.

Names of some of people shot dead at the toll gate, according to Sahara Reporters: Victor Sunday Ibanga; Abuta Solomon; Jide; Olalekan Abideen Ashafa; Olamilekan Ajasa; Kolade Salami; Folorunsho Olabisi; Kenechukwu Ugoh and Nathaniel Solomon.

PREMIER PERFORMANCE BY STUDENTS OF THE DEPARTMENT OF PERFORMING ARTS AND MUSIC, AJAYI CROWTHER UNIVERSITY, OYO (20TH JUNE, 2022)

CREW

Director – Adeeko Oreoluwa
Stage Manager – Isaac Adekitan
Sound – Praise Philip, Favour Awuzie
Props – Toni Sowande, Adams Ovie & Enioluwa Akindoju
Set – Ayomikun Onafowokan
Makeup – Michelle Eze-okeke, Inioluwa Ogundipe
Business –Eyitayo Akinwale
Costume –Henry Johnson, Etima James

CAST

Narrator – Antony Great
Funmi Agunbiade – Ojo Ayomide
Sogunle – Nwosu Michael
DPO – Phillips praise
Officer – Opadiran Kunle
Officer 2 – Ola Precious
Officer James – Adetule Toluwanimi
Boy 1, 2, 3 – Olorunfemi Fufilment, Akindoju Enioluwa, Sowande Toni
Lady – Akinwale Eyitayo

Voices – Oladeji Dorcas, Ogundipe Inioluwa, Adetunji Ayomide, Ogundeyi Happiness
Mob – Oladapo Rachael, Ojelabi Titilayo, Ogunwale Francisca, Famurewa Oluwapelumi, Akinrinola Eniola, Adeyemo Adedamola, Aremu Oluwasetemi, Oduwaye Oreoluwa, Oderinde Justus, Okere Shalom, Nasiru Kehinde, Ojo Ayomide, Sowande Enioluwa, Ekong Kingsley, Oyetola Rahman, Omoloye Eniola, Ojo Darasimi, Agbadugo Stephanie

Tableau

Light comes up on stage. It is evening on a street. There are different categories of people moving from one end of the stage to the other. Sellers of different items are strategically placed at different parts of the stage with a number of buyers negotiating. Bus conductors are also active trying to get passengers into their buses. The street is busy and lively. (The activities here reflect those of the popular Ojuelegba in Lagos after close of work or any other busy street, the director has experienced).

Four officers of the SPECIAL ANTI-ROBBERY SQUAD (SARZ/SACS/SAKS/ZIS/SCIID etc.) appear on the scene casually dressed with a SARZ crested vest jackets on. One of them fires his gun into thin air. Everyone takes to their heels, exiting the stage from different directions. Two of the policemen run after the bus conductor backstage, light flickers to heighten the mood. The once busy and lively street is suddenly empty and quiet, save for the other two officers. Goods are scattered everywhere on the stage. One of the officers picks a local gin in the usual small sachet from the littered goods on stage and gulps it down. The other brings out a stick of cigarette from his pocket and lights it. There is a very wild laughter from them as they exit the stage. **Sharp blackout.**

Narrator's First Appearance

The follow spot picks the entrance of the NARRATOR from the aisle. He is a young man in his early 20s. He is costumed as such. He walks down the aisle as he speaks.

NARRATOR: Ekaabo o, I welcome you all. The little you have seen is not the beginning of our story. No! We jumped right into the middle, but not without a proper understanding of the beginning, our history. The middle is where we are, but the end is what is important, our destination. Come with me as we find the path that leads to an acceptable destination on issues that borders around security. Come with me!

Theme song comes up. Narrator walks to the Orchestra, exchanges greetings with the players and remains there. Theme song fades out slowly.

SCENE ONE

Music from a saxophone opens the scene. The intensity of the stage lights increases with the pitch of the music. FUNMI, a young man appears on stage, he's the author of the beautiful tune we have opened with. We enjoy the dexterity and mastery of FUNMI on the sax for a while before SOGUNLE enters the stage. SOGUNLE, of the same age as FUNMI, serves us some very nice contemporary dances, which we sometimes find funny without FUNMI acknowledging his presence.
Few minutes later, FUNMI plays the last bars of the music piece. He receives an unexpected applause from SOGUNLE and members of the orchestra.

SOGUNLE: *(Clapping.)* Fantastic! Wow! Funmi-Sax my man *(Gesturing)* I doff my hat Sir (*Tapping his back playfully*)

FUNMI: *(Surprised at first but still goes on to take a bow.)* Thank you Sogun, my day one fan. How long have you been here?

SOGUNLE: Long enough to notice how much you have improved. You, my friend, are becoming a master.

FUNMI: *(A bit Flattered.)* You don't say? Well, if only I can get some chords right, I would be challenging Lagbaja and the likes you know.

SOGUNLE: Yes now, challenger of Lagbaja*(Smiles.)* Wait first, let's talk about something serious. What do you have in this house?

FUNMI: My saxophone *(shows the sax to SOGUN while still hanging on his neck)* myself, and...

That is about all. Let me just say music is all I have in this house.

FUNMI performs Ise Orin song with the members of the orchestra while

SOGUNLE *wears a disdainful look.*

ISE ORIN (APALA)

Iseorinlo'ri ran mi o /x2	I have been destined to be a musician
Emi'n se loya	I am not a lawyer
Benimi'n se Dokita	Neither am I a doctor
Iseorinnimoyan'layo	Music is my only choice

The song remains in the background.

SOGUNLE: Ekaabo! I meant food, Jor

***SOGUNLE** tries to enter FUNMI'S room but FUNMI gets up in time to block the entrance.*

FUNMI: Sogun, there is no food in this house. In fact, today is the second day of my 40 days of dry fasting.

SOGUNLE: Dry fasting? Didn't we have drinks at Jimoh's house yesterday?

FUNMI: Ehn, *(Shrugs.)* My kind of dry fasting is special. Anything fluid is allowed.

SOGUNLE: I see.
Sogunle pushes Funmi away from the door and goes in. He comes back almost immediately with a loaf of bread.

SOGUNLE: You have just confirmed to me that creative people are good liars. I thought you said there is no food in the house. What is this? *(Shows him the bread)*

FUNMI: Look at you, when you will not read your Bible. What you have there is bread to represent the Body of Christ. I'm still looking for money to buy soft drink or juice to represent the Blood. And together, I can have both as Communion in a holy and confined place where no one is present, especially you, my friend.

SOGUNLE: Say no more.

SOGUNLE *breaks the bread into two equal halves but only after doing the sign of the Cross three times and gives one half to FUNMI, who continues to watch in bewilderment.*

SOGUNLE: Here is your own share of the body…
He brings out a 50CL pet drink from his pocket, goes into the room and comes out with a glass cup. He pours some into the glass making sure that both the content in the glass and bottle are equally shared. He hands over the glass to Funmi.

SOGUNLE: … and the blood. Communion is served.
FUNMI drops the glass and quickly grabs the pet bottle

FUNMI: I want the blood in the pet.

SOGUNLE: *(Feels cheated.)* Well, I shared the drink equally. But next time, I'm getting the plastic.

FUNMI: Next time? May there not be a next time. *(He takes a big bite from the bread in his hand, takes a sip from the drink before dropping it on the floor and putting the bread on the pet as a lid. He looks more serious.)*

Sogun, how long do we continue like this? When will I blow" in this" Lagos?

SOGUNLE: Say no more. *(He drops his glass of drink and holds his bread in his mouth. He gets up to search his pocket before finally bringing out a folded paper. He passes it to FUNMI.)*

FUNMI: What is this?

SOGUNLE: Open and read young man.

FUNMI: *(Reluctantly unfolds the paper and reads from it.)* The Nigerian Police Force is recruiting?

SOGUNLE: Is that not what is in the paper?

FUNMI: Yes, it is. I'm just wondering why you gave it to me. Oh! You have decided to join the Force, fantastic!

SOGUNLE: Me? No o, who dash agbero dictionary? I brought the form for you.

FUNMI: Me? How? Will the Police Band be recruiting musicians too?

SOGUNLE: Will you be serious with your life for once? Who is talking about the Police Band? Nobody is stopping you from fulfilling your dream of becoming a great saxophonist and musician.

FUNMI: Then why are you giving me this?

SOGUNLE: Think man, you are smarter than this now. *(He moves closer to him.)* If you apply for this job and you get it, which I'm sure you will, it will change your life. Sorry, our lives.

FUNMI: Then what about my music?

SOGUNLE: *(Frustrated. His face crunches into a frown)* Think, Funmi! Your earnings will be used to promote your music and your brand. Besides, you are quick to forget the Honourable Representative in your Constituency at the Federal Level knows your family and can easily add you to his quota. You will be drafted instantly. *(Gesturing with his index finger repeatedly, hitting his head.)* Think about it FUNMI, think!

FUNMI: *(Giving it a thought.)* Hmmm… Sogun, you know this may be an opportunity for me to be a part of the system, understand the system and find ways to change the system. I think I will consider this opportunity. Maybe our Police can still be salvaged. Maybe I can be a part of those who'll change the status quo. Maybe there is hope for our Police. Maybe I can be the beacon.

The follow spot takes us back to the Orchestra, the Narrator addresses us from there.

NARRATOR: Interesting! Funmi's decision to join the Police Force is fuelled by his passion to see a Police that works for the people. For him, joining the Force is an opportunity to change the system and probably write his name in gold.

VOICE 1: He wants to change the system *(laughs uncontrollably.)*

VOICE 2: Funmi wants to change the system *(giggles.)*

NARRATOR: What a venture! An adventure indeed!
Theme song closes the scene as.

SCENE TWO

On stage left, light slowly reveals a police station. Two officers are manning the usual characteristic desk you find in a typical Nigerian Police Station. The DPO walks in while the two officers give their salutations. The DPO goes through the register on the counter. While at it, four new recruits march in and take position on one side of the stage before giving a general salutation to the DPO.

DPO: *(He drops the register.)* As you are boys.
The officers stand at ease.

DPO: The Force is proud of you young officers and how you have conducted yourselves during the period of the training.

OFFICERS: Thank you Sir.

DPO: Now, I have been directed by the State Commissioner to put the four of you into separate units of the Force. *(Points to an Officer)* For you Yemi Ajala, you will be in the P.R.O unit.

Yemi Ajala gives a well-coordinated salutation before marching off stage.

DPO: Abiodun Kyari, Prompt Response Unit.

Abiodun Kyari demonstrates good marching skills and ends it with salutation before exiting.

DPO: Mercy Ike, Force Mopol Unit.

There is a look of disappointment written over Officer Mercy Ike's face. She quickly comports herself, salutes the DPO and exits in a less ceremonious way still showing her displeasure of the posting.

DPO: Funmi Agunbiade, Force Special Anti-Robbery Squad.

TWO OFFICERS: *(Excitedly, at the desk.)* SARZ!!!

FUNMI is surprised with the reaction of the two officers at the desk but he controls himself and marches with great artistry, ending it with a perfect salute to the DPO. He makes his exit before the DPO stops him.

DPO: Young man, the Department you have been posted to is one of the best any officer can be in the Force. I expect that you make the best of this opportunity.

FUNMI: *(Standing at Attention.)* Yes Sir. I will not disappoint you Sir.

FUNMI holds his position until the DPO goes into his office. The two Officers at the desk congratulate FUNMI one after the other, with excitements written all over them.

OFFICER 1: Congratulations. You are really very lucky.

OFFICER 2: You must know some strong people. We should be friends *(He stretches his hand for a handshake.)* I'm Officer Titus. Abeg connect me 'sharperly' too now.

FUNMI: *(Confused.)* Connect you? I don't' understand what you are saying. *Wetin you mean?*

OFFICER 1: SARZ, the unit you are posted to, is a juicy unit. Many pay huge amounts to get into that Department.

FUNMI: Really?

OFFICER 2: Yes! In fact, many have described the unit as the oil block of the Nigerian Police.

FUNMI: Interesting! *(Getting more interested.)* Are there special trainings, seminars and bonuses for officers in the SARZ Department?

The two officers burst out laughing. Officer 2 raises a song. Officer one also joins, and we enjoy some choreography. (The choreographer may adopt any trending Nigerian contemporary dance, or if familiar with the ZANKU and LEG WORK dances, can create something around it.)

ORO TI O YE O SONG (ZANKU)

Oro ti o ye o loni	A conversation you don't understand today
Ounbowa ye o lola	You will come to understand tomorrow
Ogbeni lo farabale/x2	Have some patience Mr. /x2
Ounbowa ye o lola	You will come to understand tomorrow

After singing the song to their satisfaction, they bring it to a stop.

OFFICER 2: So, you see my friend, you will soon understand what we are trying to tell you.

OFFICER 1: Bros, when you start to dey understand, no forget us o

OFFICER 2: Leave am make him forget now, nawetin we do Dubem we go do am

They laugh and shake hands in a "guy code" manner.

FUNMI: Who is Dubem? And what did you do to him?

OFFICER 1: You ask too many questions, officer.

OFFICER 2: Don't worry, if you want to find out, don't do what you should.

FUNMI: I don't like the sound of that, officer. It sounded more like a threat. And to think I still don't understand you both?

OFFICER 1 walks back to his desk and gets busy with the files.
OFFICER 2 puts his hands in his pocket, whistles as he walks past FUNMI back to his position behind the desk. FUNMI is left standing and speechless.

SCENE THREE

Street. The Narrator moves from the Orchestra, as if going to the stage. Gunshot rents the air. The Narrator takes cover at the apron, and observes. Series of montages follow in quick succession using the "straight take technique". Sandwiching the actions are young boys and a girl raising placards to show the location where an action takes place. The actions are those of men of the Special Anti- Robbery Squad (SARZ), arresting and brutalizing members of the society.

MONTAGE ONE (LAGOS)

Two young adults, male, are rolling their joints, bare chest, with laptops and phones scattered on a table they have in front of them. SARZ men storm in and seize the boys just before they could escape. Prominent among the officers is Funmi. He's gentle with the boy under him while his colleague demonstrates Police Brutality on the boy he apprehended. Funmi's colleague roughly handles the boy, slapping and kicking him incessantly, cursing and using Yoruba expletives at the boy. Funmi is surprised at the handling, but says nothing.

MONTAGE TWO (KANO)

A young man, in his mid-20s, dressed in colourful clothes is walking with a young lady. Upon seeing SARZ officers, he quickly exchanges his iPhone with the lady's small, torchlight phone. The officers stopped them for questioning. After searching him and making sure that there is no other phone on him, they allow them to go. The boy and the girl share a knowing smile as they walk out earshot of the police officers.

MONTAGE THREE (LOKOJA)

Two young men, in their early 20s are standing close to a street corner, having a heated conversation about what makes a successful artist. One the guys, with a guitar strung over his neck, argues intensely with the other, same age with sagged jean trouser. SARZ officers' storm in and arrest both of them. The officers are rough with them, going as far as hitting one on the head as they drag them off the stage.

MONTAGE FOUR (ABUJA, CLUB HOUSE)

Loud music is playing. Young men and women are dancing, bodies entwined. a hype man is shouting into the microphone. Drinks. Shisha. Cash littered everywhere. Somebody from the crowd of dancing bodies scream that the DJ was doing a great job. SARZ men storm in. A few of the guys try to run, before we see one of them spraying the officers with money. The officers soon have drinks in their hands and are now enjoying the party.

MONTAGE FIVE (PORT-HARCOURT)

A well-dressed male with a crew cut, a long sleeve shirt that's perfectly tucked into a black trouser. He has a small men's handbag. He is in a hurry, so he quickens his steps, intersecting between running and walking. A SARZ officer, who is by the side of the road and saw him walk-run, stops him. The officer frowns at him before asking the man to give him his bag. The guy, in a hurry, asks the officer what the issue was.

MALE: Officer, why do you want my bag? I am late for work (He glances at his wrist watch)

OFFICER: How that wan take consign me. Oga, give me your bag now!

MALE: Officer, what do you want from my bag?

The officer drags the bag off the man's hands, opens it. As he is opening it, another officer joins him. The second officer cocks his gun as he sees the man try to collect the bag from the officer. The man withdraws his hand.

The officer finds a laptop in the bag. He shows his gun-wielding colleague the laptop. The colleague gives a cheeky smile before signalling to the man to move in a different direction.

The man refuses at first, but he soon complies after the police officer lands him a resounding slap. The man holds his stung face, and wanted to say something when another slap meets his already sore face. Both police officer pushes him into the car, slapping his back and cussing him intermittently.

Projected on the Cyclorama are newspaper headlines from different media outfits, reporting the activities of Officers of SARZ all across the country. At one side of the Orchestra pit, we have news men and women interviewing members of the community.

VOICE 1: *(Speaking to newsmen.)* We are saying that SARZ is a rogue unit and a well-organized crime syndicate that has the support of the Government. *The Narrator has found his way to the newsmen.*

NARRATOR: *(Speaking to newsmen.)* This is not the Police we want. It is not the Police we deserve. We deserve better. We demand, with immediate effect, the release of our young men and women arrested unlawfully by the Police. We are giving the Police 24 hours, if they fail to release these people, we will hit the streets in protest.

VOICE 2: *(To members of the orchestra.)* But what is our friend that wishes to change the Police doing?

VOICE 3: If you can't beat them, you join them.

NARRATOR: How are you sure Funmi has joined in the recklessness of some of our Police officers that we see very often? Funmi is our hope, he promised to be the beacon. He needs us as much as we need him. We must continue to pray for him. Funmi must not join the bandwagons!

SCENE FOUR

Action is back at the Police station, it is night. Young men and a lady arrested from the raid are filed into the cell. FUNMI walks in and goes straight to the desk. At the desk, he writes on a paper. After a while, the two Officers engage him in a chat.

OFFICER 1: Officer officer! You people had a productive night o. You are doing well *(laughs.)*

FUNMI: What do you mean?

OFFICER 2: The number of arrests you made now.

FUNMI: Oh that, we are only doing our job.

OFFICER 2: And you are doing a great job. Just make sure say the reward reach our side.

FUNMI: What reward is that?

OFFICER 1: Why are you always asking questions?

FUNMI: Shouldn't I ask questions to clarify what I don't understand?

Another officer of the SARZ unit, OFFICER JAMES, comes on stage, obviously a superior officer to FUNMI.

OFFICER JAMES: Boys, how unadey?

OFFICERS: Fine Oga

FUNMI: Very fine Sir.

OFFICER JAMES: These criminals don write statement?

BOYS: *(Shouting from the cell.)* We no be criminals…

OFFICER 1: Shut up!

OFFICER JAMES: Leave them officer, dem think say na play I dey follow dem play for here.

OFFICER JAMES walks closer to where the boys are held prisoners, and sees the lady in a separate cell.

OFFICER JAMES: *(To FUNMI.)* What is her offense?

OFFICER 1 answers before FUNMI could speak.

OFFICER 1: She be picker oga

LADY: *(Revolting.)* I am not a picker. I am an influencer. This is wrong profiling; I must call my lawyer now. *Officer 1 moves closer to the lady, and threatens to hit her, before FUNMI stops him.*

OFFICER JAMES: *(Clears his throat.)* Any of unadon ready to commot this place?

BOYS: Yes Oga

BOY 1: Officer, abeg, na me be the only pikin wey my mama get. She go don dey worry by now

BOY 2: I have a job interview tomorrow, Sir. Please release me.

BOY 3: Wetin we do sef? Why are we being locked up in this terrible place?

LADY: I want to call my lawyer!

OFFICER 2: *(Screaming.)* Shut up!!!
Everywhere is quiet.

OFFICER JAMES: *(Clears his throat.)* Well, it is easy for you guys to leave this place. All you need to do is pay some small amount for your bail.

BOY 2: Isn't bail free? *(Pointing to the mantra on the wall, boldly written on it "BAIL IS FREE".)*

OFFICER JAMES: Oh that! *(Clears his throat.)* Forget about that young man. Do you lodge in a hotel for free? Don't you pay for the luxury and facilities you enjoy?

BOY 1: *(Pointing to another mantra on the wall on which is conspicuously written POLICE IS YOUR FRIEND.)* But how Police con take be my friend if I must pay for my bail?

OFFICER JAMES moves a little more closely. There is a brief moment of silence, he stares at the boy, then snaps his fingers. The officer at the desk walks to him carrying a small bag from which he brings out a P.O.S machine and hands it over to OFFICER JAMES.

OFFICER JAMES: Young boys and lady, we accept cash, we accept transfer…

OFFICER 1: Union Bank. Account number 0224757377

OFFICER JAMES: And there is P.O.S *(showing the machine to the boys who are left dumbfounded).*

After a silence that lasted for a minute or more, one of the boys breaks the silence.

BOY 3: I will use the P.O.S, Sir. How much is my bail?

OFFICER JAMES: #20, 000 only. *(He smiles and shake hands with Boy 3.)* Now you have become a friend of the police. *(Clears his throat.)* Who else is ready to be a friend of the police?

SCENE FIVE

FUNMI'S house, SOGUNLE comes from backstage with a plate of rice and a glass of water. He sits to eat but not before FUNMI enters, obviously just returning from work.

FUNMI: I think it's high time I collected my key from you, Sogun. *(He goes to take a seat as he undresses.)*

SOGUNLE: Welcome, and good evening to you too.

FUNMI: Who is greeting this one? Are you eating?

SOGUNLE: No o, I am vomiting ni *(laughs.)*

FUNMI: I don't have your time.

FUNMI removes his shirt picks his shoes from the floor and walks inside. He soon comes back on stage with his saxophone.

SOGUNLE: I left some food for you in the kitchen.

FUNMI: Thank you. The only thing I am hungry for right now is this. *(He plays some lovely tunes and stops all of a sudden.)*

SOGUNLE: Why did you stop?

FUNMI: Excuse me?

SOGUNLE: I was enjoying your music. It was helping my food go down well.

FUNMI: May you choke on that food.

SOGUNLE: If I choke, I will drink water… *(He soon chokes on the food and quickly reaches for the glass of water. He drinks, and after a while, he stabilizes.)* You are a wizard!

FUNMI: *(It is FUNMI'S turn to have a good laugh. He quickly switches mood, as if remembering an unpleasant scenario).* Sogun, I am what, two months into this Police job and I'm tired and sick of it already.

SOGUNLE: *(Surprised.)* Tired?

FUNMI: Yes! See SOGUN, the Police job ought to be one of the most respectable jobs in this country but it is not. At least, we watch movies and read international news, we see how the Police in other countries take the job very seriously and the respect their uniform commands. Here, it just feels different. Like we are in a different world, in another universe. Which kind of Police do we have? The force is not FORCING o, Sogun.

SOGUNLE: Say no more. *(He drops his food, and jumps to his feet. He immediately enters role playing mode as he recreates scenes from American Movies, adopting accents and gestures known with the "oyinbos".)* Excuse me Sir, are you Mr. Funmi Agunbiade?

FUNMI: *(He plays along.)* Yes. What can I do for you, Officer?

SOGUNLE: We would like to invite you for questioning at the Force Headquarters. If you may, Sir *(showing FUNMI out.)*

FUNMI: Ok. Can I contact my Lawyer?

SOGUNLE: Please go ahead, Sir. It's your civic right.

SOGUNLE briskly switches into another character, this time, recreating scenes from Police Officers often portrayed in the Nigerian Nollywood. FUNMI is happy to play along.

SOGUN: Mr. Funmi Agunbiade, we have been looking for you.

FUNMI: Officer, I hope there is no problem?

SOGUN: There is problem and you will find out when you get to our station. Now move or I move you!

FUNMI: Just like that? Won't you at least tell me what I have done?

SOGUN: You will find out when you get to the station. You criminal! Move I say

SOGUN pushes and manhandles FUNMI. There is a clear show of Police brutality, call it the exact re-enactment of how Nigerian Police treat innocent citizens.

FUNMI: But Sir…

SOGUN: You have the right to remain silent for whatever you say or do shall be used against you in the court of law. Now move it young man or I …

(Players from the Orchestra echo "MOVE YOU".)

It's just the perfect time for SOGUNLE and FUNMI to enjoy some really good laughs. FUNMI cuts away from the re-enactment.

FUNMI: You see! There is not much to desire in our own Police Force when compared with other countries.

SOGUNLE: There is a salary to desire my friend. Or have you gotten another job? Ogbeni, this is Nigeria o, our ways are peculiar to us.

FUNMI: Of course! I know this is Nigeria but things are really getting out of hand. Okay. Can you believe we raided some boys and made them pay #20,000 each for bail?

SOGUNLE: *(Excited.)* Are you for real?

FUNMI: Yes now.

SOGUNLE: *(His face lightens up the more.)* How many boys were arrested?

FUNMI: Three boys

SOGUNLE: And you collected #20,000 from each?

FUNMI: Isn't that what I just said?

SOGUNLE: That is 60k in one night Funmi. A whole 60k! How can you even say you are tired of God's blessings?

FUNMI: God's blessings? How?

SOGUNLE: Calm down jor. How many officers went on the raid?

FUNMI: Three of us. Why all these questions?

SOGUNLE: You will soon understand my friend. But please, answer this last one. How much were you given?

FUNMI: My boss invited me into his office this evening and gave me #10,000…

SOGUNLE: *(Shouts for Joy.)* 10k in one night. We are made, FUNMI.

FUNMI: You didn't allow me to finish you fool.

SOGUNLE: Oh! There is more?

FUNMI: Yes.

SOGUNLE gestures to FUNMI to continue.

FUNMI: I rejected the money.

SOGUNLE: *(Has a look of disbelief written all over his face.)* You did what?

FUNMI: I rejected it.

SOGUNLE: Why?

FUNMI: Why not?

SOGUNLE: Who rejects free money?

FUNMI: Free but cursed money.

SOGUNLE: Cursed? How?

FUNMI: How not? Those boys were exploited in their own country by men who are empowered with public funds to protect them. That's how Sogun.

SOGUNLE: *(Obviously disappointed.)* I pray your holier than thou attitude doesn't make you poor for the rest of your life Funmi. Haven't you heard that one gets his meal from where he works? Or do you want to remain poor forever?

FUNMI: Legitimate meal, Sogun. Legitimate meal, not stealing and extorting people. And what I get from my salary and other small bonuses the government pays us is what God was talking about, not stealing, Sogun. What I am getting now may not be sufficient but I'm content.

SOGUNLE: Content? Who born am abeg?

FUNMI: Beyond being content is the fact that I also have integrity. I'll not soil my hands with such money. I joined the Force to be a shining light, to change the system, not be a part of the system. *(Funmi sits down and cuts a frustrated figure)*

SOGUNLE: *(Hands on head.)* Ah! "wantipada get oremi"! *(He places his left hand on Funmi's head as though he were conducting a deliverance section for him)*

FUNMI: What happened to you? Ogbeni remove your hand from my head. Which one is laying of hands, oga?
(He removes SOGUN'S hands from his head.)

SOGUNLE: You are the one something has happened to.

FUNMI: That one is your business. I sha know one thing, I'll still be richer than one person I know in this life no matter how poor I get.

SOGUNLE: And who would that be?

FUNMI: You of course!

It's time for some child's play as SOGUNLE chases FUNMI around the space for a while before running after him backstage.

SCENE SIX

Commentary from a live football game fills the air. Underneath the commentator's voice are other voices of young male passionate supporters. We can hear all the sounds and noises associated with a typical Nigerian football viewing centre. Right from backstage, through the door of the viewing centre, SOGUNLE runs on stage standing at the door of the viewing centre.
He brings out his phone from his pocket.

SOGUNLE: *(Staring at his phone.)* Some people just don't know the right time to call… *(A shout comes from the viewing centre. Bodacomot for road. We no come here come watch you.. He picks the call but not without taking a quick peep at what is happening inside.)* Hello… "Hazard score this goal now!" Hello… Yes.. I can hear you now, I dey viewing centreabeg.
He ends the call and follows it up with a long hiss. He returns the phone back into his pocket

SOGUNLE: Some people "can like" to disturb…
Shouts of "GOAL" rents the air. Fans at the viewing centre are hitting tables and chairs and hugging each other's sweaty bodies. SOGUNLE runs inside while the noise continues before running

back outside immediately shouting goal and then returning back inside with exhilarating joy. As the shouts and roars subside from the viewing centre, the regular Siren that announces the Nigerian Police is heard. Boys from the viewing centre run to the stage and exit in different directions.

BOY 1: AK

BOY 2: Na SARZ o

Two men of the SARZ unit, dressed in Police Uniforms, the SARZ vest on, with guns in their hands run after four boys from backstage to the stage. One manages to escape and narrowly misses a bullet from the SARZ officer's gun. They apprehend three of the boys. SOGUNLE is among the three guys arrested. The boys try to explain their case to the officers, one of them saying they were only watching football. One of the police officers, the one with a bald head, yells at him to shut up if not they would regret opening their filthy mouths.

SARZ OFFICER ONE: *(Brutalizing the boys.)* Criminals! Bring out your phones.

SARZ OFFICER TWO: *(Collecting phones with force. He uses the butt of his gun to hit SOGUNLE, who is reluctant in giving his phone.)* Give me the phone now. *(He collects the phone)*

The Officers go through the phones for a while.

SARZ OFFICER ONE: *(As if noticing something criminal on the phones.)* Ah! What app is this?

You guys are Yahoo boys. I will deal with you today.

BOY 1: Yahoo? No *(He brings out his ID card.)* I work with the Federal Broadcasting Cooperation…

Officer snatches the ID card from him.

SARZ OFFICER ONE: *(Looks at the ID with contempt.)* You are a media man?

BOY 1: Yes! I am a journalist.

SARZ OFFICER TWO: And so what? Do you think we will be afraid of you?

SARZ OFFICER ONE pulls his colleague to a corner for a quick aside but still keeping an eye on the boys.

SARZ OFFICER ONE: This one na bad market o

SARZ OFFICER TWO: How now oga?

SARZ OFFICER ONE: All these media people can be full of wahala. Small thing now, we don see our faces for newspapers. And this wan wey be say small thing na social media, we no need this kind market.

SARZ OFFICER TWO: No be say dem even get money sef. Abeg, make we discharge am before him spoil business for us.

They end the aside and return to the boys.

SARZ OFFICER TWO: *(Returns ID back to Boy one.)* Go before I change my mind.

BOY ONE collects his card and runs out of the stage. SOGUNLE gets up and follows him. SARZ OFFICER TWO pulls him back. He tries to release himself from his claws. The scene becomes a little rowdy. The tussle continues for a while before SARZ OFFICER ONE joins. After the long pushing and shouting, the rifle in the hand of one of the Officers triggers. We see SOGUNLE shot in the stomach, and slowly goes to the ground. when the SARZ officers see SOGUN's corpse on the ground in the pool of his blood, they run out of the stage, leaving the other boy. The boy, seeing what happened, cries out in pain. Thinking his life has been spared, the boy looks up, in hope of thanking his maker for sparing his life, only to see the menacing look of one of the officers, who shot him directly on the head. The boy's body thumps on the ground, letting out a soft, painful cry. The officer who just shot the boy runs off the stage, never staring back at the two dead bodies.
Dirge instrumental music comes up from the orchestra.

NARRATOR: I don't even know what to say.

VOICE 2: Say anything
He is now on stage, looking at the lifeless bodies of SOGUN and BOY 3.

NARRATOR: They had dreams.
The dirge now rents the air, and members of the orchestra come on stage to take the bodies out.
Lights fade out slowly.

SCENE SEVEN

At the Police station, there is only one of the Officers at the desk, writing in a book. FUNMI walks out of what seems to be the DPO's office with anger. He walks past the desk before the Officer calls him back.

OFFICER 1: Ah! You no wan greet us today, Officer?

FUNMI: *(Stops in his tracts.)* You all deserve to rot in hell.

OFFICER1: *(Surprised.)* Excuse me? *(He drops his pen and steps away from the desk to a more open place just by the side of it.)* Officer Funmi, what is the problem? Why are you fuming this early morning?

FUNMI: The entire Police Force is what is wrong with me. *(He unbuttons his uniform.)* Anyone who wears this cursed uniform is not better than the devil. *(He removes the shirt, drops it on the desk.)* I'm done here. I just dropped my resignation letter in your Oga's office.

OFFICER: Have you lost your head? How dare you disrespect the badge and ranks of the Force?

FUNMI: How dare the Force kill my best friend?

A moment of silence that lasted for about one minute takes the atmosphere. After which FUNMI breaks into serious tears.

FUNMI: I am the only child of my parents. SOGUN came into my life and changed that narrative. I found a brother in him. He got me the Force form, encouraged me to join the Police, and use my salary to fund my Music. It's a shame that the same Force he advised me to be a part of took his life in that way and manner.

OFFICER: *(Moves to pet him.)* These things happen, officer; please don't take a rash decision. Why not apply for a short leave, take some time to think it through maybe…

FUNMI: *(Picks himself up.)* There is no thinking this through. How do I continue to serve in the same Force that killed my only brother? What do I say to his one-year-old daughter when she grows up and ask me who killed her dad? His parents, what eyes will they use to look at me? And will I ever forgive myself for not being able to defend my friend and brother when he needed me the most? If you find answers to these questions, maybe, just maybe you can then convince me about thinking my decision through.

VOICE 3: So sad.

VOICE 2: This is the end of that dream.

VOICE 1: What dream?

VOICE 2: Officer Funmi's dream to change the Police.

NARRATOR: The end? Why must this be the end of that beautiful dream? It is fine if Funmi can't carry on with it, and it is understandable too. But what about the rest of us? There must be something we can do. This shouldn't be the end of our dream to have a Police that will truly be our friend. This can't be the end. We must make it the beginning of the next phase of Funmi's dream.

VOICE 1: And what is this next phase?

NARRATOR: The phase where we, members of the society also get involved. The phase where we demand security from armed officers, especially members of SARZ. Let us at least do this for Sogun. Who knows, it might be any of us tomorrow, or our children.

VOICE 2: For Sogun

ORCHESTRA: For Sogun!!!

The dirge surges up. FUNMI sorrowfully walks out of the stage in the tempo of the song.

SCENE EIGHT

A different day. Light comes on stage. FUNMI is sitting in a corner looking so sad. He looks up, and looks down. His eyes roam the stage, as though he were looking for what wasn't there. Then he cups his face in his hands, head bowed in silence for a few seconds. He raises his head, looks at his saxophone that rests lazily at one corner of his room. After a long stare, he picks himself up, walks to where the saxophone is placed. He feels the saxophone with his hands, caresses it, and picks it up. He places it close to his mouth, plays for sorrowful sound for a few seconds, and breaks down in tears. His eyes are wet with tears, and his hands tremble with the saxophone. He plays for a few more seconds before dropping the saxophone. He sits on the chair, head raised, eyes staring into nothingness.

FUNMI: Why? Why did it have to be Sogun? My Sogun!
He breaks down in tears again. A voice comes from the Orchestra.

VOICE ONE: How long will you continue this way, Funmi?

FUNMI: For as long as it takes.

VOICE TWO: SOGUN is gone forever.

FUNMI: I know he is. I know I will never see him again to argue with. *(Sobs)*

VOICE TWO: Oh, you do. So what will you do about it? Sit here and sob? Will you let your friend die for free? By the hands of the unit you work with? Is that how much you.

FUNMI: Stop! Stop it! I miss Sogun. I miss him. I don't want his death to be for nothing. I want it to mean something.

VOICE ONE: We miss Sogun too. But what will you do, FUNMI? What will you do? *The voice chides him till FUNMI breaks down in tears again.*
FUNMI sobs even loudly.

VOICE ONE: We know it hurts that you couldn't protect him.

VOICE THREE: It must hurt badly. But you can prevent this from happening to someone else.

FUNMI: *(Cleans his tears and suddenly seems interested.)* How?

VOICE ONE: By using your voice.

FUNMI: I have a voice?

VOICE TWO: Everyone has a voice.

FUNMI: Really? What voice do I have?

VOICE THREE: Music! Your voice!! Your Voice, FUNMI!!! Use your voice for SOGUN's sake, at least.

ALL THREE VOICES: Use it /x3

FUNMI picks up his saxophone; he moves downstage and looks straight at the members of the Orchestra. Some hope is restored on his face.

FUNMI: If I decide to use this voice of mine, will you my friends help echo it?

ORCHESTRA: Positive. We will echo your voice. Positive!!!

FUNMI: Roger that.

FUNMI'S spirit is now lifted. He jumps down the stage and joins the Orchestra that has every member now standing. He plays harmonious sounds from the sax which the Orchestra choruses. It's a performance of a series of freedom songs. Different set of dancers comes from the Orchestra to perform short but energetic dances to each of the music. While the songs and dances are on, there are those from the Orchestra recording the events and taking pictures of the happenings with their gadgets.

PROTEST SONG ONE (Calypso)

When shall we be free? /x2
Free from SARZ and all
When shall we be free?
We want Freedom
Oh Oh … Freedom.
Freedom from shame and maim
Freedom from pain and death
We want freedom
Oh Oh… Freedom

PROTEST SONG TWO (HIP-HOP)

Enibamo won kowi fun/x2	Let the one that knows tell them
Won yiote o	They shall be disgraced
EgbeSARZ	The SARZ cult
EgbeApayan	The cult that kills
Won yiote o.	They shall be disgraced

PROTEST SONG THREE (AFRO BEAT)

CALL (SAX): A rararara	Fela's signature call
RESPONSE (ORCHESTRA):	
O roro Response to Fela's roro/x2	
ALL: Dem peme/x2	They killed us

Peme peme peme peme peme	Killed us/x5
Dem peme	They killed us
CALL: Dem peme our youth o	They killed our youths
RESPONSE: Peme	Killed us
CALL: Dem no wan make we grow	They wouldn't let us grow
RESPONSE: Peme	Killed us
CALL: Same people wey we know	
The same people we have always known	
RESPONSE: Peme	Killed us
CALL: Those wey suppose protect	Those who should protect us
RESPONSE: peme	Killed us
CALL: How we wan relate..ti	How do we fathom this?
RESPONSE: Peme	Killed us
CALL: Dem say Youth na leaders	They told us youth are leaders
RESPONSE: peme	Killes us
CALL: Leaders of tomorrow	Leaders of tomorrow
RESPONSE: peme	Killed us
CALL: Wetin we never see	What have we not seen?
RESPONSE: Peme	Killed us
CALL: Wetin we never hear	What have we not heard?
RESPONSE: peme	Killed us

CALL: For this countirry eh In our country
RESPONSE: Peme Killed us
ALL: Dem peme Killed us
Peme peme peme peme peme Killed us/x5
Dem Peme
They killed us

The last song transits into a dirge with hums accompanying instrumentals. Lights dim almost immediately. Two men carry the corpse of SOGUN right across the apron. FUNMI makes an attempt to follow the corpse but members of the Orchestra stop him. This scene is tense and sorrowful. Everyone watches as the corpse is being carried out while a flute plays in the background. Light fades slowly before going off completely.

SCENE NINE

Action is back at the Police Station. The two officers on the desk are engaged with their phones such that they didn't notice the entrance of the DPO. The DPO observes them for a while before calling their attention by the usual clearing of the throat.

OFFICERS: *(Dropping their phones and throwing salutations in the air as many times as they could.)* Shun Sir!

DPO: Remain like that.

OFFICER 1: Sir?

DPO: I said hold your positions. That is your punishment for getting carried away with your phones while on duty.

OFFICER 2: Oga, you certainly have not heard.

OFFICER 1: Neither have you read.

OFFICER 2: Or see.

OFFICER 1: And neither has it crossed your mind what FUNMI is doing.

DPO: Who is FUNMI?

OFFICER 1: *(Whispering.)* Ask Google

DPO: Pardon?

OFFICER 2: Officer FUNMI, formerly of the SARZ unit Sir.

DPO: Oh! That self-righteous guy, yes, what about him? What did he do this time?

OFFICER 1: Sir, you will need to check INSTABLOG on Instagram, Sir.

OFFICER 2: INSTABLOG carries fake news. Oga, please check SUB DELIEVRY ZONE on TWITTER Sir.

OFFICER 1: You are a fool. No SOCIAL MEDIA platform gives gist like Instablog.

OFFICER 2: Says who? Even Instablog is on Twitter now.

OFFICER 1: Says me and fellow Nigerians

OFFICER 2: Y'all must be fools.

OFFICER 1: Including Oga?

OFFICER 2: Is Oga part of you people?

OFFICER 1: Is Oga not a Nigerian?

OFFICER 2: Well then…

DPO: I am a fool right?

OFFICER 2 quickly goes down on his knees. While OFFICER 1 finds the whole scene funny but try to control his emotions.

OFFICER 2: *(On his knees)* I am sorry Sir. What we are trying to say is that Officer FUNMI has gotten into the heads of the people on the street. And the people are now staging a protest against the Force.

DPO: Protest? Where? When?

OFFICER 2: *(Now back on his feet.)* On the Social Media Sir.

OFFICER 1: They have created #tags such as **#ENDSARZ #NOTOPOLICEBRUTALITY #REFORMNIGERIANPOLICE** and many others.

OFFICER 2: The campaign is gaining prominence Sir. And many people are joining FUNMI to discredit the Nigerian Police Force.

DPO: You don't say? Well, nobody will take any online campaign or protest seriously. Nigeria hasn't reached that stage yet…
His phone rings.

DPO: *(Perplexed.)* It is the CP. *(Speaks into the phone.)* Morning Sir, CP Sir, yes… my boys just told me now Sir… Yes Sir! I'm on it immediately Sir… Yes… that FUNMI boy and his team will be dealt with… I will give you a detailed report before 6 PM Sir… Shun Sir.

The DPO ends the call.

DPO: I was wrong. The news has gotten to the CP already.

He walks straight into his office while the two officers follow him.

SCENE TEN

At the Orchestra pit. FUNMI leads in a mob of angry young men and women singing songs of protest. It's a peaceful march against Police Brutality and the call for the Government to end the operations of the SPECIAL ANTI ROBBERY SQUAD (SARZ). The protesters carry different placards with different messages boldly written on each. Messages such as – POLICE HAS BECOME OUR ENEMY #ENDSARZ, STOP POLICE BRUTALITY #REFORMNIGERIPOLICE, STOP KILLING THE YOUTHS, STOP DESTROYING OUR HOPE OF A BETTER FUTURE #ENDSARZ. (These are some of the messages on display; however, the director can add more of such messages that show the people's displeasure against the FORCE, especially SARZ.)

FUNMI: *(Climbs the stage to address the people who by now have broken into a group of two, holding positions on both sides of the apron. They bring the song down just as he makes to speak.)* My people, I thank you all for your doggedness and forthrightness so far. It is not over until we win, until the Government listens to us and reforms or scrap the SARZ unit of the Nigerian Police Force.

VOICE 1: Non-negotiable. *(Raising his placard high up above his head with an utmost sense of responsibility.)* #ENDSARZ.

FUNMI: Thank you, my people. I want to beg us, not to relent. Let us keep the fire burning, let us keep demanding for the immediate shutdown of the culture of impunity within the Police force and a total reform of this charade we call the Police Force. Let the conversation continue online and offline. Let's get the #tags trending. Let us show them that times have changed.

VOICE 2: *(With phone in his hand, obviously recording the event.)* We are live on all Social Media platforms. Our #tags are number one on Nigerian trends. The whole world is watching.

FUNMI: *(Delighted.)* Thank you, this is pleasant news.

VOICE 3: Wait till I tell you how Nigerians in the Diaspora have also been joining us in the protest.

FUNMI: Really? I'm sure the Government must be feeling the heat now and as a result will do the needful.

MOB: *(Shout for joy.)* Eh Eh

FUNMI gets his sax, plays some good music while the people sing and dance along. There is a general sense of victory in the air. After some few minutes, over and above the music, we hear the sirens from police vehicles. The scene becomes rowdy as some of the mobs run in different directions trying to find an escape. FUNMI is seen still holding his position, waiting for the worst to happen. Some men of the Nigerian Police enter, and arrest FUNMI. Action freezes on stage as the Narrator speaks from the aisle.

NARRATOR: Animals! Speaking of animals, the difference between man and animal is choosing when to respond to danger. We want to solve this problem, but on our phones. We are afraid to die. Can SARZ kill us all? When do we get to the breaking point? When do we say enough is enough? Where are those shouting no to Police Brutality just now? We all should have stayed to stop these officers from arresting Funmi. We are more than them! But we don't want to die. We say this country is not worth dying for. So we have abandoned Funmi, forgetting that none of us is safe, even in our homes.

Action resumes back on stage. The officers take FUNMI out of the stage as light slowly fades.

SCENE ELEVEN

Light resumes back at the Police station. One of the officers usually on the desk brings in FUNMI to the stage. Just as FUNMI, who is now at the desk, makes to write his statement, the DPO walks in while the second officer who would usually be at the desk carries a bag obviously belonging to the DPO right after him.

DPO: *(To the officer on the desk.)* Morning

OFFICER: *(Standing at attention.)* Shun Sir!

DPO: As you are. Has he written his full statement now? *(Pointing to FUNMI.)*

OFFICER: Yes Sir!

DPO moves closer to FUNMI who is at this point done writing and just leaning on the desk. He breeds confidence.

DPO: FUNMI, what is wrong with you? How would you gather people against an institution that once fed you?

FUNMI: *(Smiles.)* An institution that fed me you say? DPO, can I ask you a very simple and honest question?

DPO: Yes Funmi. Please go ahead.

FUNMI: How long have you been in the Force?

DPO: *(Boastful.)* That is a very good question. Next year, I will be 27 years in the service.

FUNMI: Very good. In your 27 seven years in the Force, have we ever had it this bad?

DPO: Well, I don't know what you mean by *(imitating FUNMI)* "have it this bad". However, I can boldly tell you that we have never had it this good. And with this government, we will even have it better until we have the best. That is why your actions are a bit strange to me. I thought you were bright. How can anyone quit a Police Job in a time like this? Haven't you heard of the juicy salary package this administration has just approved for men of the Force?

FUNMI: Has the new package changed anything? Has it reduced bribery among you and your men?

DPO: It is yet to be implemented, son. Once it is, you will see how the Force will wear a different look.

This is why I think you should stop all the nonsense you are doing. Your resignation letter is still on my table. Take your job back and be of service to your nation

FUNMI: *(Getting Emotional.)* Take my job back? You mean I should take back the same job that killed my best friend and made her daughter fatherless even before she gets to know him?
The DPO places his hand on FUNMI's shoulder who immediately shrugs it off. The DPO is surprised and quickly keeps his hand to himself.

DPO: FUNMI, we all know that was only a mistake.

FUNMI: You called killing a man a mistake?

DPO: It was an accidental discharge. Don't let sentiments get the better of you. Stop showing you are emotionally weak; you are a man.

FUNMI: (Angry) Emotions have got nothing to do with gender.

DPO: Really? You are a disgrace to all men.

FUNMI attacks the DPO. The two officers quickly stop him before he gets really violent.

DPO: *(Adjusting his uniform.)* Lock him up. And add physical assault of an officer to his charges.

The officers drag FUNMI out as lights go off.

SCENE TWELVE

NARRATOR: *(Walks down from the isle. As he speaks, members of the orchestra are seen moving to the apron one after the other.)* Today is the day. Today is the day we take our protest back to the streets. Today is the day we demand the release of Funmi and others that have been arrested and locked up unjustly. Today is the day we use our numbers to fight and win this course. Today is the day we take back our country from the oppressors! We will no longer be oppressed in Nigeria! We are done!

All members of the orchestra are now at the 2 sides of the apron, protest song takes centre stage. The song gets louder as the lights come back on stage to light the Police Station. The two officers are on the stage, perplexed. DPO comes out from backstage, which is assumed to be his office. The DOP looks confused and angry. He looks at the two officers at the desk, and growls at them with his stare.
The protesters bring down their songs so we can hear the conversation on the stage.

DPO: Where is that noise coming from?

OFFICER 1: From protesters, Sir.

DPO: What are they doing in my station?

OFFICER 2: About five thousand of them are outside, sir. They say you must release FUNMI today, Sir.

DPO: Five thousand people?

OFFICER 2: Yes, sir.

OFFICER 1: Don't mind him Oga. They are not up to five thousand Sir.

OFFICER 2: I counted them.

OFFICER 1: When?

OFFICER 2: When you were busy hiding behind your desk.

OFFICER 1: How dare you?

DPO: Shut up you both! I wonder how you both got into the Force.

OFFICER 2: *(Aside.)*The former Minister of Defence is my uncle.

The song comes up again from the protesters. They are at this point making serious noise with their songs and stamping of feet. The two officers run down stage, look towards the apron and run back to their position where the DPO is still standing.

OFFICER 1: They will bring down the station's gate if we don't act now, Sir.

DPO: What am I supposed to do? Go out there and try to pacify them?

OFFICER 1: Maybe. You will have to speak to them if not all of us in the station are gone. My wife is heavily pregnant, I can't die now o.

DPO: Shut up there! *(To OFFICER 2.)* Go and get me the megaphone in my office

OFFICER 2 runs backstage and runs back on stage almost immediately with a megaphone which he hands over to the DPO. The DPO walks down stage, stops right at the tip with the two officers standing at a considerable distance away from him. He addresses the protesters.

DPO: Fellow citizens of our great country

One of the protesters signals that they stop singing and listen to the DPO. The noise reduces drastically so we can hear the DPO.

DPO: My name is MAKIN BAKU, I'm the DPO of this station. Please calm down and tell me why you are here.

VOICE 1: We demand the release of FUNMI SAX.

DPO: I am sorry, but the law does not work that way. There are several charges against FUNMI and it is only the court of law that can at this point determine what happens to him.

VOICE 2: Charges? What are these charges, we want to know.

ALL: Yes. We want to know.

DPO: It is my duty to tell you. The first charge against FUNMI is disturbance of public peace.

VOICE 1: How?

DPO: By organizing and leading a protest.

VOICE 2: Does our law not allow for peaceful protests anymore?

ALL: Ask him o.

VOICE 3: Or have you people killed him like you do people you don't like?

VOICE 4: There is nowhere in the constitution where protesting is breaking the law.

VOICE 1: Ok. What is the second charge, we want to know.

ALL: Yes. We want to know.

DPO: Your self-acclaimed freedom fighter, FUNMI, assaulted an Officer of the law.

VOICE 3: When?

VOICE 4: Who is the Officer?

DPO: Yesterday. Only yesterday. And I am that officer.

VOICE 3: How did he assault you?

VOICE 2: You people are known to tell lies, so what evidence do you have that he assaulted you?

DPO: I don't need you to believe me, the court of law will answer all your questions. And for the other leading a protest, the court of law will answer your questions

ALL: Lies. We demand that you release FUNMI to us now!

DPO: I cannot do that. You don't determine what is law around here, the court does.

VOICE 1: Then we will not leave this place until you grant our wish.

DPO: It is in your best interest that you leave. If you don't, you'll bear whatever happens to you.

ALL: Nothing will happen to us. We are Nigerians, and we can't be oppressed in our country.

DPO: Nobody is oppressing you. I am saying leave here and let the law do its work.

ALL: Chants *We No Go GREE o.*

VOICE 3: How many of us can you and your boys kill?

The DPO is even more surprised by the resilience of the group. He calls the two officers close, as if having a deliberation with them while the protesters resume their songs, this time moving very close to the stage but still at the apron. The DPO and the two officers are afraid of the crowd but try very hard not to show it. The DPO leaves for his office while the two officers follow him. He stops just before he enters his office, and they also stop. He enters his office and quickly shuts the door before they could enter. They hold on to the door begging the DPO to open. Light goes off slowly.

SCENE THIRTEEN

At the Police Station, the voice of the Vice – President comes up in a radio broadcast. As we listen to the Vice- President's speech, FUNMI is being released and all his properties returned to him. (The director should artistically work the lines from the broadcast to the actions at the Police station perfectly.)

VICE – PRESIDENTS BROADCAST (To be recorded).
Following persistent complaints and reports on the activities of the Special Anti-Robbery Squad (SARZ) that border on allegations of serial violation of fundamental human rights, I, as the Vice-President, and also in my capacity as the acting president hereby direct the Inspector General of Police with immediate effect, to overhaul the management activities of SARZ. I have also directed that all citizens who are unlawfully detained should be released immediately and be allowed to return to their family members. God bless the Federal Republic of Nigeria.

There is a loud shout of victory from the Orchestra. They run to the stage and lift FUNMI shoulder high. They place him down amidst the singing that is now accompanied by well-choreographed Nigerian contemporary dances. After the songs and dances, FUNMI addresses the joyous crowd.

FUNMI: Thank you, thank you and thank you everyone. If we celebrate more than we are doing today, it is worth it. This victory today is for my very good friend SOGUNLE AREMU and many other Nigerian youths who have lost their lives to Police brutality and recklessness in service delivery. Let this be the start of a social revolution in our nation. The government and all its agencies exist today because the people exist. With technology and social media, let us demand good governance, let us demand good policing from our Police Force. We are a courageous people, and courage does not shiver at the face of adversity. The achievement of this historical milestone isn't the end. We can do more and should do more. I call for more unity, kindness, and singularity of voice as Nigerians. We can and will change the narrative as Nigerians. Let us all be good citizens of our country. I thank you all once again for your resilience and spiritedness over this menace. The Special Anti-Robbery Squad (SARZ) thought they were SACROSANCT but we have shown that no institution of the government is…

VOICE 1: *(Pressing and reading from his phone.)* Breaking news… The president has sacked the Inspector

General of Police and has appointed another person as the IG with immediate effect.

ALL: Eh *(All shouting for joy)*

FUNMI: My people, I am sorry to cut short your joy. But I hope this is not fake news? There are too many fake news flying around on social media these days. We must always verify the source.

VOICE 2: *(Also reading from his phone.)* The news is confirmed o. Another reputable media organization just reported the same news. In fact, it says the new IG is giving his first press conference as we speak.

FUNMI: Can we stream the press conference online?

VOICE 2: I don't have data

ALL: *(Disappointed.)* Ah

VOICE 1: I have data. Come around everyone

The entire mob moves closer to VOICE 1 who now has his phone in his hand in a horizontal position. The crowd forms an arc around him while he takes the center next to FUNMI. We can hear the audio of the visual they are seeing.

INSPECTOR GENERAL OF POLICE (IGP) SPEECH

… I thank the President for this appointment
I promise we shall consolidate on the achievement
of my predecessor and work hard to reform
the Nigerian Police Force. With the permission of
the President however, I hereby return men of
the Special Anti-Robbery Squad unit (SARZ) back
to their status-quo…

ALL: (Surprised.) Ah!

As the speech continues to go on in the background, FUNMI raises a song.

SONG

For us, nothing is changing
For us, our story is starting a new
When shall we be free? /2ce

The rest of the mob joins him as they exit the stage one after the other. A young boy is left with FUNMI on stage and as he also makes to leave, FUNMI stops him and hangs his Saxophone on his neck. He holds him by the hand and they exit the stage.

NARRATOR: While you are here, some young men and women are being harassed by SARZ officers. Your son, friend or relative may just have escaped these men by luck today, will they escape tomorrow? Who talk say as you dey drive home now SARZ no go stop you for road?

Shebi you know say Police go still stop your bike? Remind me of how many Police checkpoints dey before you reach your house again? Tonight, we have journeyed through a path we thought will lead us to our expected destination. However, this destination can't be the destination. It means one thing; that our destination, our Jerusalem, where there is no Police Brutality, Extrajudicial killings, Extortion, Manhandling is still far ahead. Our true destination will be a reformed Police Force. Until we get there, we will not rest. In the meantime, we must change this mentality of "e no concern me".

Light goes off but comes back on immediately in its full intensity. The boy we saw with FUNMI takes the Centre stage learning how to play the sax. This is before us for a minute or more before a sharp blackout.

THE END

www.ingramcontent.com/pod-product-compliance
Lightning Source LLC
LaVergne TN
LVHW041229150826
845673LV00008B/2330

* 9 7 8 9 7 8 7 6 9 8 0 0 6 *